To Deryk, with love
—L.S.

To all my teachers and mentors, especially Vasil Madzlin,
Gayle Crom, Bernard Cody, and Ron Dresslove—
I'm still reaping the fruits of your labors
—D.M.

Where's God?
Text copyright © 2003 by Dr. Laura Schlessinger
Illustrations copyright © 2003 by Daniel McFeeley
Printed in the U.S.A. All rights reserved.
www.harperchildrens.com

Library of Congress Cataloging-in-Publication Data
Schlessinger, Laura.
Dr. Laura Schlessinger's Where's God? / Laura Schlessinger ; illustrated by Daniel McFeeley.—1st ed.
p.   cm.
Summary: When Sammy tries to look for God with his binoculars, his grandfather explains where and how to find God.
ISBN 0-06-051909-6
[1. God—Fiction.   2. Grandfathers—Fiction.]   I. Title: Where's God?   II. McFeeley, Dan, ill.   III. Title.
PZ7. S347115 Dr   2003   [E]—dc21   2002005646   CIP   AC

1 2 3 4 5 6 7 8 9 10
❖
First Edition

Dr. Laura Schlessinger's

Where's God?

Illustrated by Daniel McFeeley

HarperCollins Publishers

"Sammy! Sammmyyy!" called Grandpa. "Where are you, Sammy? It's time to come in for dinner! Grandma's got your favorite supper on the table! Sammy! The biscuits are hot—don't keep 'em waitin'!"

"I'm up here, Gramps!" answered Sammy.

"Well, what are you doing there with the binoculars, Sammy?" Grandpa asked. "It's too light outside for stars."

"I'm not looking for stars, Gramps. I'm trying to find God," said Sammy.

"Why are you trying to find God?" asked Grandpa.

"I want to talk to God, Gramps," said Sammy. "I need to ask Him for a big favor. I want Him to go to the hospital and help Mommy's knee get better so she doesn't need surgery and can come home right away."

"Oh," said Grandpa, "so you think you need to find God before you can pray to Him to help your mother?"

"Yeah," said Sammy, "I think it's like calling someone on the phone. I have to know where they are so I can dial the right number. If they're not where I'm calling—I won't get to talk to them."

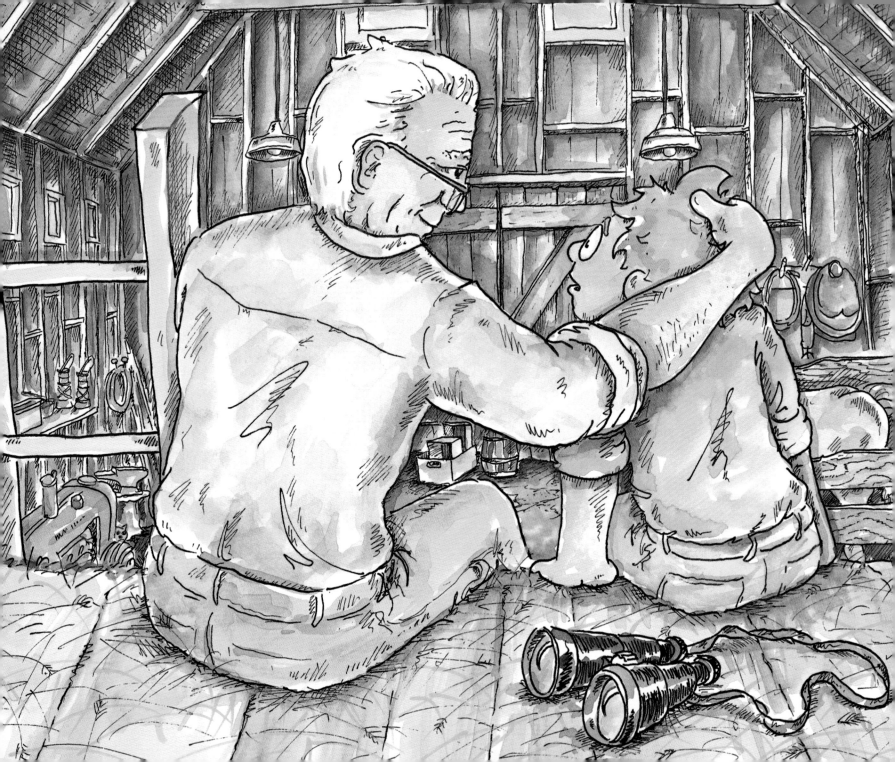

"Who told you that you had to know exactly where God is before you can talk to Him?" asked Grandpa softly.

"Nobody," Sammy said proudly. "I figured it out myself. One time when I asked God to get me out of trouble so Mommy and Daddy wouldn't be mad at me, He didn't do it. So I figured He couldn't hear me 'cause He wasn't where I was praying."

"I see," Grandpa said, cleaning his glasses thoughtfully. "You think God didn't do what you wanted because He wasn't where you were when you were asking for His help? So now you're going to track Him down before you pray—so that for sure He'll do what you ask of Him?"

"Yup, Gramps, that's exactly right," said Sammy.

"Sammy, where have you looked?" asked Grandpa.

"Well," said Sammy, "I asked just about everybody where God was. It was weird—everybody had a different answer.

"The grocery man showed me his fruits and vegetables and said God was in all growing things. That made me feel funny about eating my salad.

"The mailman pointed to the hills and sky and said that God was in the beauty of all things on the earth—but weeds aren't beautiful, so I got confused.

"The kid at the candy store said God was in church on Sundays, and that's why you have to be quiet in church—because God doesn't like too much noise.

"Miss May at the pharmacy said that God was in people helping one another—but some people do some bad things. What about that? Where's God then?

"Then I heard a preacher on TV say that God is up in heaven. I figure that means He's in the sky. I wonder what holds Him up. Does He sit on clouds? When there are no clouds in the sky, does that mean that He's moved somewhere else?"

"Sammy," said Grandpa lovingly, "everybody kind of told you the truth. God created the earth, so everything is part of God—even the weeds—because everything has a purpose and a beauty, even if we don't always understand what or how or why.

"God created people, and we all have the goodness of God in us—and we can choose to be good the same way we can choose to be bad. God is in us just the same, loving us and being patient as we get back on the good track."

"I can kind of see what you're saying, I guess," said Sammy slowly. "But now I don't know what to do. How do I find Him and talk to Him and get Him to listen and give me my wish?"

"Sammy, my boy," said Grandpa reassuringly, "you must understand two things. You think that God didn't hear you pray to Him to get you out of trouble after you did something wrong. Well, Sammy, He did answer you. He let you get punished because you earned that punishment and needed to learn from it.

"Sometimes God's answer is no—but there's always a good reason. Sometimes it takes growing up to understand the reason. Sometimes it's just too hard to understand. But you must trust God."

"Gramps," whispered Sammy, "God might say no to fixing Mommy's knee? Why would He do that?"

"Sammy," said Grandpa, "God's answers and God's help are not always as fast and simple as we might like them to be. God *is* helping your mother. He's doing it through the good doctors who are helping her. God is also expecting your mother to help Him help her by doing the exercises she needs to do to make her leg strong. God works through all of us."

"So if God is in me, then I already always know where He is, and I can talk to Him anytime?" asked Sammy.

"Right, Sammy," said Grandpa, smiling.

"Gramps, please tell Grandma I'll be right in for supper," said Sammy happily. "I have to talk to God first."

"Okay, Sammy. I love you," said Grandpa.

"I love you, too, Gramps," Sammy answered.